3 4028 08057 4347
HARRIS COUNTY PUBLIC LIBRARY

JPIC Agee
Agee,
The ot   W9-BJK-370

WITHDRAWN $17.95
ocn812534715
1st ed.   11/06/2012

THE OTHER SIDE OF TOWN

JON
AGEE

MICHAEL DI CAPUA BOOKS | SCHOLASTIC

COPYRIGHT © 2012 BY JON AGEE • LIBRARY OF CONGRESS CONTROL NUMBER: 2011935782 • SCHOLASTIC, NEW YORK, NY 10012 • PRINTED IN SINGAPORE 46 • FIRST EDITION, 2012

I was having a lousy day—few fares, bad tips, a flat tire—when this guy in a funny hat waved me down.

"Take me to Schmeeker Street," he said.

"You mean *Bleecker* Street, downtown?"

"No, *Schmeeker* Street, on the other side of town."

He told me how to get there, past the bus depot and the city dump, till we came to a dead end.

"Here we are," I said. "This must be the other side of town."

"Not yet," he said, and he whipped out a remote control and pressed a button.

The wall in front of us opened.

"What's this?" I said.

"The Finkon Tunnel."

"You mean the *Lincoln* Tunnel, after Abe Lincoln?"

"No," he said, "the *Finkon* Tunnel, after Gabe Finkon. He's famous on the other side of town."

"Okay," I said, "let's go."

The Finkon Tunnel went on for miles.

I looked back and noticed the guy was reading the sports pages.

"You like baseball?" I asked.

"Yes," he said. "I root for the Spankees."

"You mean the *Yankees*?"

"No, the *Spankees*. They're the best team on the other side of town."

The tunnel let out onto a maze of ramps.
"Straight ahead," said the guy, "and look out for spotholes."
"You mean *pot*holes?"
"No, *spot*holes. Everybody complains about them on the other side of town."

I swerved and hit a spothole. Everything went black.

"Don't panic," he said. "You just need to turn on your nog lights."

"You mean *fog* lights?"

"No, *nog* lights. Don't you have nog lights?"

"No, I don't. But let me guess—everybody has nog lights on the other side of town."

Then—KA-THUNK—we popped out of the spothole right onto Schmeeker Street!

"What's going on?!"
"It's mush hour," he said.
"You mean *rush* hour?"
"No, *mush* hour. It's a big headache on the other side of town."

We made it through mush hour.
"There's my house," said the guy, "on the right, next to the glom tree."

He paid his fare and started to go.
"Wait!" I said. "How do I get back to the city?"
"Easy," he said. "You take the Snooklyn Bridge."
"You mean the *Brooklyn* Bridge?"
"No, the *Snooklyn* Bridge. It's the most amazing
bridge on the other side of town."

"Thanks," I said, and I hit the gas.

Well, he was right. The Snooklyn Bridge
was pretty amazing.

So amazing that it suddenly disappeared!
Everything went black.
I panicked. *"Help! Get me out of here!"*

I looked around the cab for a map. In the backseat, I spotted the guy's remote control.

There were two buttons, ENTER and EXIT. I pressed EXIT.

Presto! There was Times Square!
I hopped in my cab and raced home. I couldn't
wait to tell everybody where I'd been.

"You're just in time for dinner," said my wife.
"We're having tweet loaf."
"You mean *meat* loaf, with gravy?"
"No, *tweet* loaf, with *bravy*. It's very popular on the other side of town!"